MW00909874

WHO'S IN MAXINE'S TREE?

Text copyright © 2006 Diane Carmel Léger

Illustrations copyright © 2006 Darlene Gait

All rights reserved. No part of this publication may be reproduced or transmitted in any form or by any means, electronic or mechanical, including photocopying, recording or by any information storage and retrieval system now known or to be invented, without permission in writing from the publisher.

Library and Archives Canada Cataloguing in Publication

Léger, Diane Carmel, 1957-

Who's in Maxine's Tree / Diane Carmel Léger; illustrations by Darlene Gait.

ISBN 1-55143-346-X

1. Nature conservation--Juvenile fiction. I. Gait, Darlene, 1968-

II. Title.

PS8573.E46149W46 2006   jC813'.54   C2005-906522-2

First published in the United States 2006

Library of Congress Control Number: 2005935952

Summary: A giant Sitka spruce and an endangered seabird protect each other from extinction.

Orca Book Publishers gratefully acknowledges the support for its publishing programs provided by the following agencies: the Government of Canada through the Book Publishing Industry Development Program (BPIDP), the Canada Council for the Arts, and the British Columbia Arts Council.

Design and typesetting by Lynn O'Rourke
Interior and cover artwork created using acrylic paint.
Scanning by Island Graphics, Victoria, British Columbia

Orca Book Publishers
Box 5626 Stn. B
Victoria, BC Canada
V8R 6S4

Orca Book Publishers
PO Box 468
Custer, WA USA
98240-0468

Printed and bound in Hong Kong
Printed on 50% recycled Sustainable Forestry Certification matt art paper.
10 09 08 07 06 • 5 4 3 2 1

To Eddie and Maxine,
who have left the nest.
—D.C.L.

To my father,
who taught me so much about our forest
and inspired my love of creating art.
—D.G.

Author's acknowledgments

I wish to thank professional climber and researcher Stephanie Hughes, who provided me with information. In 1992, she climbed the 79-meter (260-foot) Maxine's Tree in the Walbran Valley on Vancouver Island and discovered the marbled murrelet nest. At the time, it was one of only five marbled murrelet nests found in Canada and one of thirty found in the world.

Thank you to Carmanah Forestry Society founder Syd Haskell, who contributed inspirational photographs of his trail building in the Walbran Valley.

I am also grateful to Wet'suwet'en hereditary chief Ron George, who suggested that I write about this incredible find as a sequel to *Maxine's Tree*.

Who's In Maxine's Tree?

story *by* Diane Carmel Léger

illustrations by Darlene Gait

ORCA BOOK PUBLISHERS

Maxine bit her lip and stared at her hiking boots.

Her cousin Eddie was staring out the car window at the clear-cut hillsides, but Maxine couldn't bear to look. What if her favorite tree in the Walbran rain forest had been cut down? What if it never called to her again?

Maxine was seven years old. She had already helped to save a giant tree in the Carmanah Valley, but what if putting a sign on the tree wasn't enough this time?

When they finally arrived at the Walbran Valley trail, the four adults and two children stretched their stiff legs and took deep breaths of the pure air. In single file, they hiked along the boardwalk, crossed the narrow bridge and climbed the stairs along Fletcher Falls.

Their first stop was Emerald Pool. Maxine took off her boots and socks and dipped her toes into the water.

"Cool," Eddie said and did the same. "Whoa!" he yelled, pulling his feet out again. "That's not cool! It's freezing!"

Maxine did not laugh with the others. She was looking at new clear-cuts in the nearby hills. Would her tree be safe?

Soon they came to a wooden box hanging in a tree at the edge of a creek, a cable car built by students from Victoria High School. Maxine's father stepped in the box and pulled the ropes like a clothesline until he reached the other side. Eddie and Maxine waited for the empty box, climbed in and bobbed across. One by one, the squished adults-in-a-box followed.

On they went along the slippery trail, over a bridge and through a stand of lumpy, bumpy cedars. Then they came to two big hemlocks that intertwined and formed a gigantic hollow. All four adults and two children walked into the tree cave. There was lots of room for more.

"Cool," said Eddie.

Down the trail a bit, Eddie shouted, "That tree looks like a real elephant! There's the head, the ear and the trunk! It even has a tusk! That is the coolest tree so far!"

Maxine grinned. "Wait till you see my favorite tree," she said.

Stomachs were grumbling when, at last, they arrived at the section of trail the grown-ups were going to clear of fallen trees. It was time for lunch, but first, Maxine had to check on her tree. Eddie followed her. He stopped beside her as she gazed up at the giant tree, the tallest and widest Sitka spruce in the whole Walbran Valley. A sign propped among the roots said "Maxine's Tree."

"Why is this your favorite, Max? It's huge, but it doesn't have a cave or low climbing-branches. Why didn't you choose the elephant tree or a hollowed cedar?"

"This is the best tree for me," Maxine said slowly. "It's the biggest and … it makes special sounds sometimes."

"A tree? Trees don't talk!"

"That's not what I mean, Eddie," Maxine said.

"Sorry, Max. It's a good tree. Hey, let's go eat."

"I'll be there in a minute," she said.

Maxine leaned on her tree and listened for the sound that she had heard before. Except for rustling branches, the tree was silent.

"Hello," a voice said.

Maxine jumped and looked up to see a woman standing in front of her, laden with ropes and equipment. "Hi!" the woman said again. "Where did you come from?"

Maxine stared at her and pointed to the bend of the trail. "I'm with the trail builders. We want to save the trees. This one is my favorite," she said and stared some more. "Who … who are you?"

"My name is Stephanie. I'm a tree climber," the woman said. "I'm researching mamu nests."

"What's a mamu?" asked Maxine.

"Its real name is marbled murrelet, but I like to call it mamu. It's an endangered seabird."

"Why are you looking for seabird nests in the forest?" Maxine asked.

"Because this is where mamus nest, deep in old-growth forest." The woman looked at the sign in the roots of the tree. "Are you Maxine?" she said.

Maxine did not answer. She had a question of her own, a very important one. "What do they … the mamu … sound like?"

The woman opened her mouth and stretched her lips. "Keer, keer," she said.

Maxine smiled. "That's the sound that my tree calls to me," she said.

Stephanie looked up, up into the branches of the tree. She looked down at Maxine. Then she took her crossbow off her back.

"Don't worry," she said. "I won't hurt the tree. I'm just going to climb up and take a look."

Stephanie shot her ropes high into the tree. Maxine watched her climb the ropes and disappear among the tree's branches. Just then, Eddie came round the bend in the trail.

"Hey, Max, you're missing lunch," he said. Then he saw the ropes. "What's going on?" he asked.

Her words tumbling out of her, Maxine told him all about Stephanie and the seabirds who made their nests in ancient trees. "They need wide branches to land with their wide webbed feet," she finished.

"Cool," Eddie said. "Let's wait."

When Stephanie came down at last, her face shone like the sun. "I found one," she said, "one of the best samples of a mamu nest I've ever seen! And I've climbed trees from California to northern British Columbia!"

"Are there baby mamus in the nest?" asked Maxine.

"Oh, no. I would never climb when the mamus are nesting."

"How do you know it's a mamu's nest?" asked Eddie.

Stephanie took a container of dirt and feathers out of her pack and opened the lid to show them. "Because I found their feces in the nest."

"What's a fe …" Maxine started.

"It's mamu poo," Eddie said quickly.

"Oh," Maxine said.

Stephanie hugged her. "Well," she said, "nobody is going to cut down a tree where mamus nest."

Maxine's happiness filled her so full that it squeezed tears out of her eyes.

"You did pick the coolest tree after all, Max," said Eddie.

They were halfway down the trail to tell the others when Maxine stopped. "I'll be back in a minute," she said.

Maxine turned around and ran up the trail and around the bend to her tree. She peered up to see the nest but saw only the dark green maze of branches gently swaying. She listened for a *keer* but heard nothing except the sound of branches dancing in the wind.

"Thank you, mamus, wherever you are. Come back soon," she whispered.

Author's Note

The marbled murrelet is a small, threatened seabird of the
Pacific Coast of North America. The size of a robin, it flies up to
70 kilometers inland to nest on the moss-covered branches of
giant conifers, which means it can travel 140 kilometers daily
to feed its young. The biggest threat to this species is loss of
habitat due to the logging of old-growth trees.